Just the Two of Us

Just the

SChOLAStiC INC.

New York Toronto London Auckland Sydney
Mexico City New Delhi Hong Kong Buenos Aires

Two of Us

by WiLL SMitH

WiTH PiCtURES bY

kADiR NELSON

This book is dedicated to my parents, Willard and Carolyn Smith, and to the memory of Grandmother. WE LOVE YOU, "GIGI"! Special props to all of the fathers out there holdin' it down. Stay strong! —W. S.

For my Mom, Emily, and my Dad, Lenwood. I love you. —K. N.

JUST THE TWO OF US (WILL SMITH RAP)
Words and music by Ralph MacDonald, William Salter, Bill Withers. Copyright © 1980, 1997 Antisia Music, Inc. (ASCAP)/Cherry Lane Music Publishing Company, Inc. (ASCAP)/Bluenig Music (ASCAP) Worldwide rights for Antisia Music, Inc. administered by Cherry Lane Music Publishing Company, Inc. All Rights Reserved · Used by Permission

ISBN 0-439-66943-X

12 11 10 9 8 7 6 5 4 3   6 7 8 9/0

Printed in the U.S.A.   40

First Bookshelf edition, February 2005

The artwork was rendered with pencil and oil paint.
Book design by David Saylor

i **TOLD MY PARENTS** I wanted to build a castle in the sky.
"Here's a pencil and paper, let's draw the plans," they replied.

I told my parents that one day a queen would wear my ring.
They said, "The only way to marry a queen is to be a king."

I told my parents I wanted to kick lil' Reggie's butt.
They replied, "Let's say that you do . . . then what?"

I told my parents I'm 17; I'm getting married 'cause I love her.
They replied, "We won't fight you if you can tell us her favorite color."

I told my parents I'm not going to college; I wanna rap.
They said, "Wherever you go, remember one day you'll go back."

I told my parents I was going to be the next Bill Cosby, funny and rich.
They replied, "Why not just work hard and be the first Will Smith?"

I told my parents I'm about to be a father and I'm scared.
They replied, "Sometimes all you need to do is simply be there."

My son told me he wanted to build a castle in the sky.
"Here's a pencil and paper, let's draw the plans!" I replied.

— WiLL SMitH

FROM THE FIRST TIME the doctor placed you in my arms

I knew I'd meet death before I'd let you meet harm.

Although questions arose in my mind, would I be man enough?

Against wrong, choose right and stand up?

From the hospital that first *night*

It took an hour just to get the car seat in *right*

People driving too *fast,* got me kind of upset

Got you home *safe,* placed you in your bassinet.

That night I don't think one wink I slept

As I slipped out of my bed, to your crib I crept

Touched your head gently, I felt my heart melt

'Cause I knew I loved you

more than life itself.

Then to my knees,

and I begged the Lord please

Let me be a good daddy,

all he needs.

Love, knowledge, discipline too

I PLEDGE MY LIFE TO YOU.

Just the two of us,

building castles in the sky.

Just the two of us,

you and I.

FIVE YEARS OLD, you're bringing comedy

Every time I look at you I think man, a little me

Just like me, wait and see, you're gonna be TALL

It makes me laugh, 'cause you got your dad's EARS AND ALL.

Sometimes I wonder what you're gonna be

A general, a doctor, maybe an MC.

I wanna kiss you *all the time*

But I will test that butt when you cut out of line.

Why'd you do that?

I try to be a tough dad, but you keep making me laugh

Crazy joy when I see the eyes of my **baby boy.**

I pledge to you, I will always do

Everything **I CAN**

To show you how to be a MAN.

Dignity, integrity, honor and

I don't mind if you lose, as long as you came with it

And you can cry,

there **ain't no shame in it.**

It didn't work out with me and your mom

But yo, when push comes to shove

You were conceived in love.

So if the world attacks, and you slide off track

Remember one fact, I've got your back.

Just the two of us,

building castles in the sky.

Just the two of us,

you and I.

IT'S A FULL-TIME JOB to be a good dad

You've got so much more stuff than I had.

I've got to study just to keep with the changing times

"101 Dalmatians" on your CD-ROM.

See me — I'm trying to pretend I know

On my PC where that CD goes.

But yo, ain't nothing promised, one day I'll be gone

Feel the strife, but trust life does go on.

But just in case, it's my place to impart

One day some girl's gonna **break your heart.**

And ooh there ain't no **pain** like from the opposite sex

It's gonna hurt **bad,**

but **don't take it out on the next.**

Throughout life people will make you **mad**

Disrespect you and treat you **bad.**

Let God deal with the things they do

'Cause **hate in your heart will consume you too.**

Always tell the **truth**, say your **prayers**

Hold doors, pull out chairs, **easy on the swears**

You're living proof that **dreams come true**

I love you and I'm here for you.

Just the two of us,

building castles in the sky.

Just the two of us,

you and I.

Daddy loves *you!*

Daddy loves *you!*

for the rest of your life.